To the students of

Hickory Grove

Bill Martin

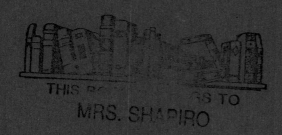

Foolish Rabbit's Big Mistake

by Rafe Martin

illustrated by Ed Young

G. P. Putnam's Sons
New York

For Rose, Jacob and Ariya   R M

This is for Ann Beneduce,
for her generous support over the years   E Y

Text copyright © 1985 by Rafe Martin.
Illustrations copyright © 1985 by Ed Young.
All rights reserved. Published simultaneously in Canada.
Printed in Hong Kong by South China Printing Co. (1988) Ltd.
Book design by Nanette Stevenson.
Library of Congress Cataloging in Publication Data
Martin, Rafe.
Foolish rabbit's big mistake.
Summary: As all the animals panic and flee at little
rabbit's announcement that the earth is breaking up, a
brave lion steps in and brings sense to the situation.
1. Children's stories, American.   [1. Animals—Fiction.
2. Fear—Fiction]   I. Young, Ed, ill.   II. Title.
PZ7.M364185Br   1985   [E]   84-11665
ISBN 0-399-21178-0

5   7   9   10   8   6

Foolish Rabbit's Big Mistake is a traditional Jataka tale or story of one of the Buddha's earlier births. More than a thousand years ago, hundreds of such Jatakas or "birth stories" were recorded from a truly vast oral tradition and so were preserved for us today. Jataka tales like this one have been told, performed, sculpted, and painted throughout Asia for nearly 2500 years.

In the West, the Jatakas are considered to be one of the great storehouses of folklore and story. They have even been cited as probable sources for both *Aesop's Fables* and *The Arabian Night's Entertainments*. This particular story is, perhaps, the oldest version of the familiar "Henny-Penny," "Chicken-Little," or "Sky Is Falling" story.

Foolish Rabbit's Big Mistake is, of course, a story about fears and rumors. As a storyteller, I find it to be a particularly effective story for reaching young audiences. They like the story's rhythmic quality. They like to identify with the brave lion who decides not to run but to help. And they like to laugh at the foolish little rabbit who discovers that his fears are literally groundless. There is real wisdom in such laughter, too. To have the courage to face what most terrifies us and be able, ultimately, to laugh at it, is, after all, the stuff of literature and of life itself.

This particular version of the tale has been recreated as a picture book for young readers (and listeners). It is adapted from the telling that I presented in fuller form in *The Hungry Tigress and Other Traditional Asian Tales* (Shambhala/Random House).

R M

Early one morning a foolish little rabbit lay sleeping under a tree in the forest. Sunlight shone through the leaves, warming the earth, and the little rabbit began to stir.

As he drifted contentedly between waking and sleeping, a foolish thought crossed his mind. *What if the earth broke up?* The little rabbit sat up, now wide awake. "What if the earth broke up today?" he said out loud. And the foolish little rabbit began to listen for signs of danger.

CRASH! He heard a loud sound behind him. And without looking around, the little rabbit jumped up and ran off, yelling, "The earth is breaking up! The earth is breaking up!"

Soon he passed another rabbit. "Say, what's the hurry? Why are you running?" the second rabbit asked. But the little rabbit just shouted out, "The earth's breaking up! The earth's breaking up! Run for your life." And he sped by.

"The earth's breaking up? Oh, no!" cried the other rabbit, and away he ran after that first little rabbit. They passed a third rabbit. "What's happen-

ing?" the third rabbit called out. "The earth's breaking up!" they panted. "Run." And run he did.

Now the three rabbits passed a sleepy bear. The bear stretched and rubbed his eyes. "What's going on? Why are you running?" he asked. "Stop and tell me." But the rabbits just kept on running and shouting, "The earth's breaking up! Run. Run."

"The earth's breaking up," repeated the bear, confused. "The earth's breaking up? Why then, I'd better get going." And the bear started running too. Soon they came upon a second bear. He was chewing a piece of dripping honeycomb and batting at the bees buzzing all around him. "Hey, what's going on? Why are you running?" he asked.

"The earth's breaking up! That's why we are running!" they yelled as they ran past. "Run. Run."

The bear scrambled to his feet. "The earth's breaking up?" he said to himself. "Oh, my gosh! There's no time to lose." And pushing the last of the honeycomb into his mouth, he started running too.

Farther along in the forest an elephant with half-closed eyes stood resting beneath a large shade tree. His huge ears fanned slowly back and forth, and his tail flicked, this way and that, sweeping off the droning flies. Suddenly his ears fanned forward and stopped. His eyes opened wide. Three frightened rabbits and two panicked bears burst through the bushes. "What's going on?" he trumpeted in surprise. "Why are you all running?"

But the terrified animals only shouted, "The earth's breaking up. Run for your life!" And they were gone.

"The earth's breaking up," rumbled the elephant. "Why, if the earth's breaking up, there's no time to lose. I'm going with you." And trumpeting wildly he too charged off, his tail pointing straight out behind him.

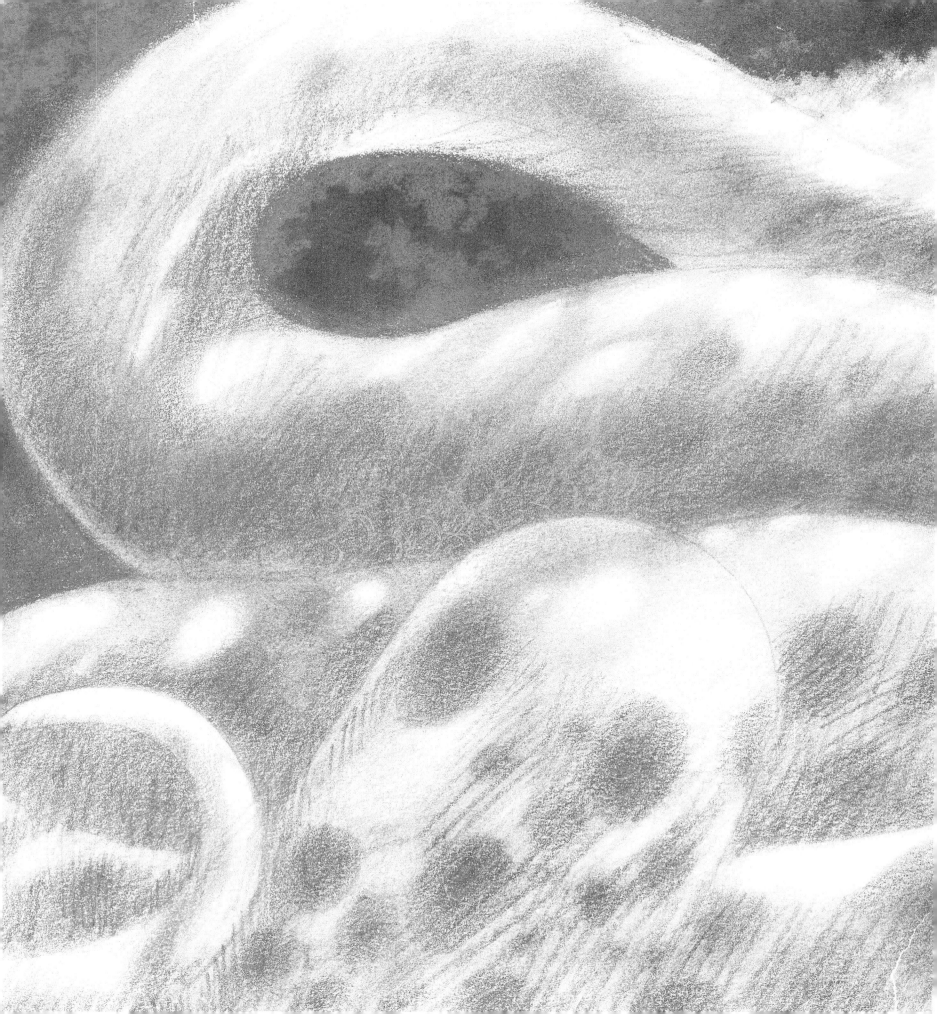

The animals ran along the path. The pounding of their feet disturbed a snake sleeping on a warm rock ledge in the midday sun. He opened one eye. He opened the other. He flicked out his sharp, pink tongue and lifted his smooth scaled head. Suddenly three screaming rabbits, two moaning bears and a trumpeting elephant stormed past.

"What'sss happening?" hissed the snake anxiously. "Why are you all running?"

"The earth is breaking up," cried the animals. "It's the end. Run for your life!" And they were gone.

"What?" said the snake. "The earth'sss breaking up? Why I'd better get sssliding." And uncoiling himself, he glided down from his warm ledge and slid rapidly after the others.

He passed another snake and another and another. When they heard what was happening, they too slid over boulders, under bushes, and around trees, following the other terrified animals. Soon an awful hissing, trumpeting, moaning and screaming filled the forest.

Now up on a mountaintop overlooking this forest was a brave lion, asleep. The lion heard all the noise. He opened his golden eyes. Looking out over the forest, he saw the animals running, running, running. He couldn't see why they were running but he could see that unless someone stopped them they would run right over the edge of a cliff and be killed. "Someone should help them," the lion said to himself. "Why, I'll help."

He rose to his feet and shook his heavy mane. Gathering his strength, he took a tremendous lion leap, waaay out, and landed in front of the terrified animals, who came screeching and panting to a sudden halt.

"RAAARRRGGGHHH!" roared the lion. "What is the matter? Why are you running?"

"The earth's breaking up! The earth's breaking up! That's why we're running," shouted the animals. "Oh, let us go, mighty lion, before we are killed."

"The earth isn't breaking up, you silly creatures," the lion said. "Look. Here's the earth solid as it's ever been." And he struck the ground a blow with his paw to prove it. "Who told you that the earth was breaking up?"

"It wasss the elephant," hissed the snakes.

"The bears," trumpeted the elephant.

"Rabbits," moaned the bears.

"It was *him,*" shouted the rabbits, pointing to the foolish little rabbit.

"Well, little rabbit, where did you see the earth breaking up?" the lion asked in a gentle voice.

"Back there under the apple tree. I heard it," stammered the foolish little rabbit.

"Hmmm," said the lion to himself. "He heard it? And under an apple tree?" Then he had an idea.

"Come," he said. "Get on my back. We'll go together and find out what it really was that scared you."

"Oh, no," protested the little rabbit. "It's too dangerous. I can't go back there." And he wouldn't move.

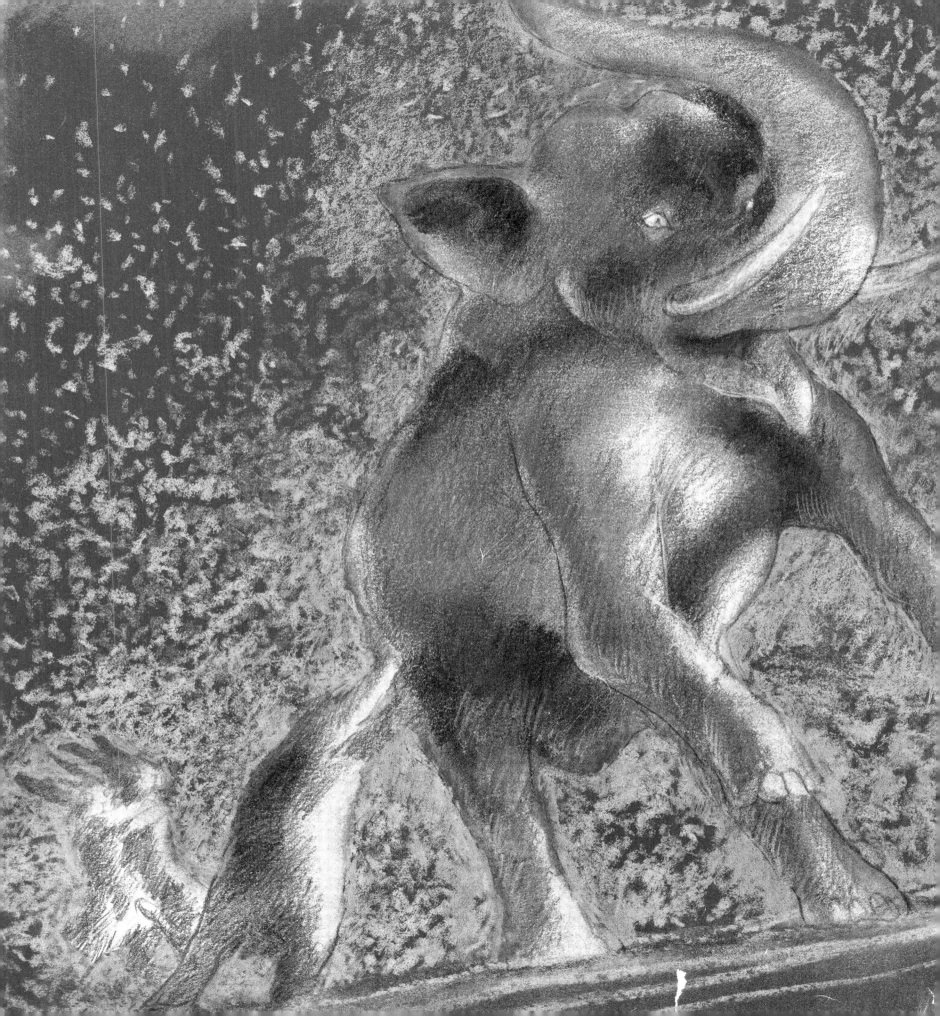

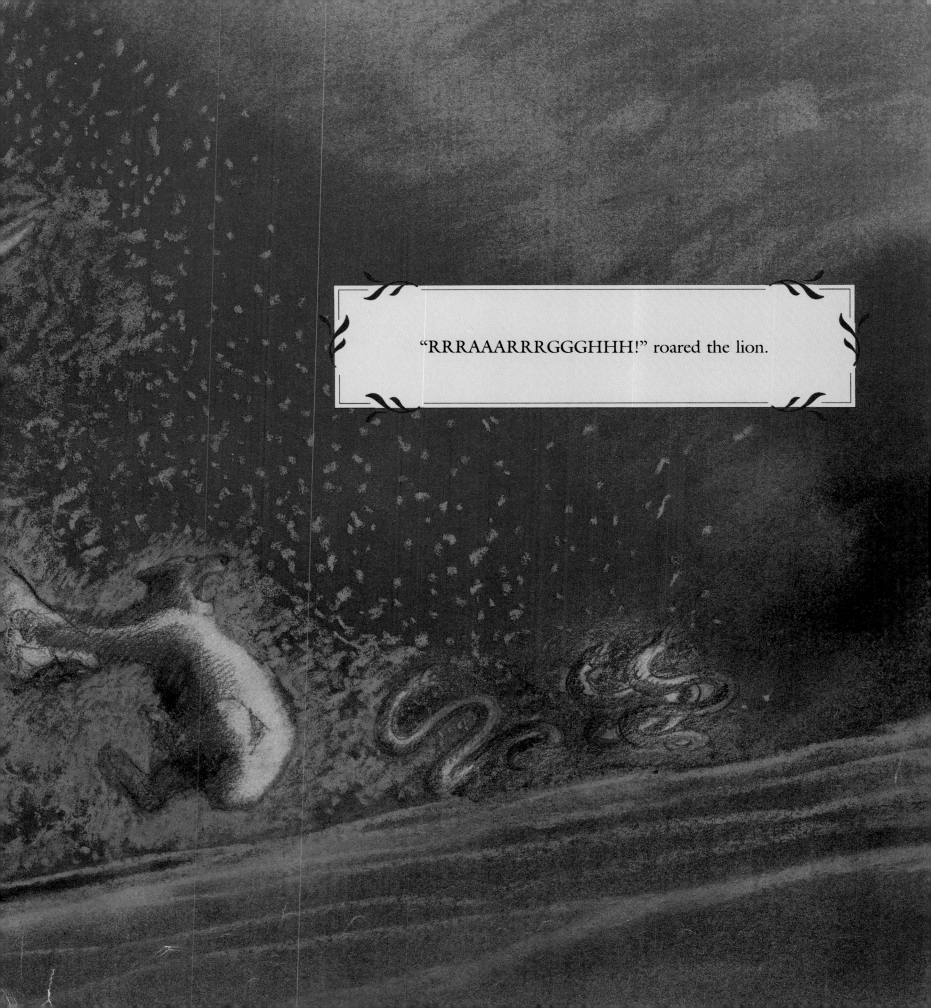

"RRRAAARRRGGGHHH!" roared the lion.

Then the rabbit said, "OK, I'll go!" and jumped up on the lion's back. The lion took one, two, three tremendous lion leaps back to the tree. He stalked around sniffing the earth. At last he found what he was looking for. There under the tree lay an apple that had fallen from the branches above.

"There's your earth breaking up, silly little rabbit," he said. "You heard this apple hit the ground and thought it was the earth breaking up."

"Oh, my," said the rabbit. "What a mistake. What a fuss over nothing."

"Well," the lion said, "we must go back and tell the others." Once again the lion took one, two, three tremendous leaps. When they stood before the animals once again, the little rabbit tried to explain. "It seems that I've made a terrible, uh, mistake. You see this apple? Well, I thought the sound it made when it fell to the ground was, um, the sound of the earth breaking up. You can all understand that, uh, can't you?"

The animals looked at one another. Then they looked at the little rabbit. "No!" they shouted at last, and they got so angry they wanted to tear the little rabbit to pieces.

"RRRAAARRRGGGHHH!" roared the lion. "Wait. You all ran without finding out what was frightening you. Remember that, next time something scares you. If you'll only stop and see what it is, you may find out that there's nothing really to be afraid of at all."

"Why, you're right," said all the animals. "Next time we'll do that."

"Me too," said the little rabbit.

Then the lion took a leap back up onto his mountaintop. He lay down, calmly surveyed the peaceful forest below, yawned and went back to sleep.

The little rabbit, still holding the apple, hopped back to the tree. He lay down beneath the branches, sighed contentedly, and took a big bite of the apple.

And that's the end of the story.

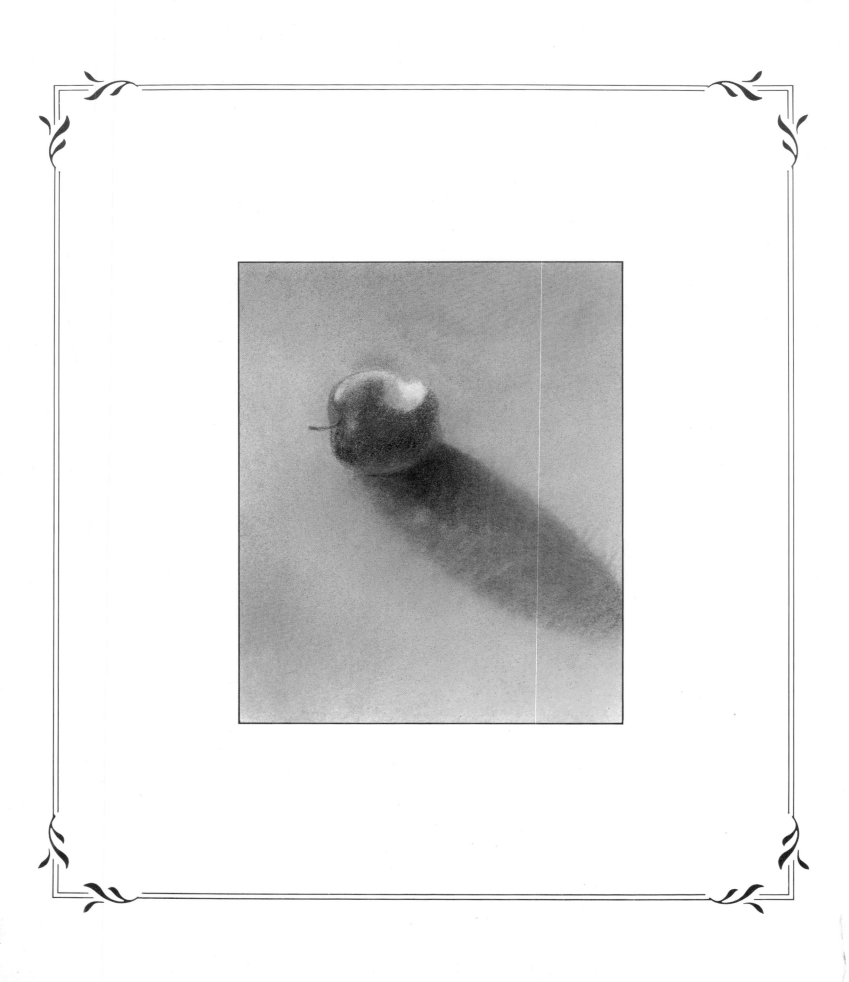